ALADDIN AND THE
MAGIC LAMP

Afterword by:
Betty Jane Wagner
Chair, Humanities Division
National College of Education

Library of Congress Number: 79-27304

3 4 5 6 7 8 9 10   96 95 94 93 92 90 88 87

Printed and bound in the United States of America.

Library of Congress Cataloging in Publication Data

Daniels, Patricia.
  Aladdin and the magic lamp.

  (Raintree fairy tales)
  SUMMARY: Retells the adventures of Aladdin who,
with the aid of a genie from a magic lamp, fights an
evil magician and wins the hand of a beautiful
princess.
  [1. Fairy tales. 2 Folklore, Arab] I. Art,
Temple. II. Aladdin. III. Title. IV. Series.
PZ8.D188Aj   398.2'2   [E]   79-27304
ISBN 0-8393-0257-6 lib. bdg.

RAINTREE FAIRY TALES

ALADDIN AND THE MAGIC LAMP

Retold by Patricia Daniels
Illustrated by Temple Art

Raintree Childrens Books
Milwaukee

I n an eastern land, in a time now forgotten, lived a boy named Aladdin. He and his mother were very poor. They lived on what work they could get in the city.

One day a man came up to Aladdin. "Aladdin, my boy!" he cried. "I am your long-lost uncle! I have come back from my travels to take care of you."

Aladdin did not know that the man was really an evil magician. The man gave Aladdin and his mother many gifts.

"But the best gift is in a cave outside the city," said the magician. Aladdin went with him to the cave. It had an entrance that only a child could crawl through.

P ut on this magic ring," said the magician. Aladdin thought this was strange, but he put on the ring and entered the cave. Inside were fabulous jewels and shining gold. In one corner was an old lamp.

"Quick, give me the lamp!" cried the magician. But Aladdin suddenly knew that he was an evil man, and held on to the lamp.

The magician was so angry that he closed up the cave and left Aladdin to die. For days Aladdin had no food or water. He looked at the magic ring, and rubbed it to see it better.

Suddenly a strange, ghostly figure appeared in front of him. "I am the genie of the ring. What is your wish?" it asked. Aladdin asked to be taken home, and so he was.

Aladdin's mother was happy to see him, but she soon became sad again. "We have no food, nor money to buy any." At this Aladdin remembered that he still held the old lamp.

"Perhaps we can sell this at market," he said. His mother took up a rag to polish it. When she started to rub, a great cloud rushed out and formed into a huge creature.

"I am the genie of the lamp," it said. "What is your wish?"

Whatever they asked for, the genie would bring them. From that time on they had all the riches they needed.

T he years passed, and Aladdin fell in love
with the beautiful daughter of the Sultan.
The genie gave Aladdin some wonderful
jewels, and he sent his mother to the Sultan's
palace with them as a gift.

The Sultan was so impressed that he agreed to
let his daughter marry Aladdin.

And yet, when the Sultan had the jewels, he began to have doubts.

"Who is this Aladdin?" he asked himself. "Where is he from, and why have I never heard of him?"

He called Aladdin's mother back the next day. "My daughter is a princess, and must live in a palace," he said. "Only if your son has a palace, may he marry her."

When Aladdin heard this, he summoned the genie.

"I must have the grandest castle ever built," he said. "It should be fit for the most beautiful princess in the world."

And the genie created a shining, jewelled palace, the like of which had never been seen in the land. Aladdin and the princess were married there the very next day.

Meanwhile, the evil magician had heard about Aladdin. He knew Aladdin must have the lamp.
"It's *my* lamp," said the magician to himself. "I must take it back."

One day when Aladdin was gone, an old peddler appeared beneath the palace windows. "New lamps for old!" he cried. "New lamps for old!"

Hearing this, one of the servants ran out with the old lamp she had always seen about the palace. Happily, the magician took the magic lamp and gave her a new one.

When Aladdin returned, his palace and wife had both disappeared.

"Find my daughter," cried the Sultan, "or you shall die!" Without his lamp, Aladdin felt lost. Then he remembered his magic ring.

The genie of the ring appeared. "But I am not so strong as the genie of the lamp," he said. "Still, I can show you where your wife and palace are hidden." And with those words he took Aladdin to an African jungle. In it stood his palace, with his wife weeping at the window.

When the princess saw Aladdin, she called out, "Oh, my love! The magician told me you were dead. He wants me to marry him, and I have no power against him."

"Do not worry," said Aladdin. "I have a plan."

Later that day, the princess called to the magician. "I have decided to marry you," she said. "Let us drink to our happiness." And she held out a glass of poisoned wine.

As soon as he drank it, the magician fell to the floor. The magic lamp fell from his coat.

Aladdin and the princess were taken back to their own land. From that time on they lived happily together. And though they had many riches, the old lamp held the place of honor in their palace.

With your finger follow the path Aladdin must take to get the magic lamp. Some clues from the story will help you on your way.

START

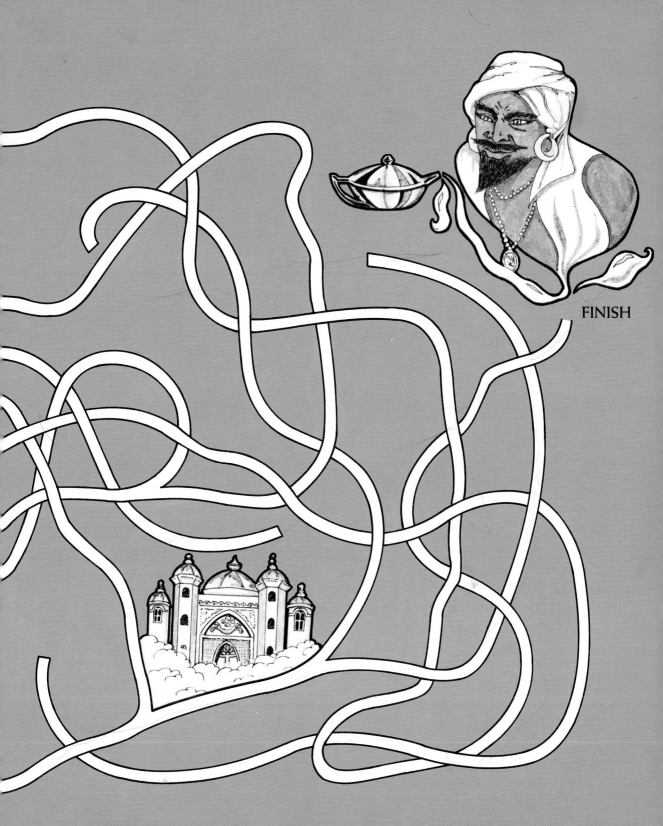

FINISH

(For the answer, turn to the last page.)

The Story of Aladdin

"Aladdin" was told long ago in ancient India, North Africa, Syria, and Persia. This story, like all folk tales, was told for hundreds of years before it was ever written down. When Moslem people gathered in coffee houses and in bazaars, one of them would entertain the others with the tale of Aladdin. No one knows who first made it up, but someone who heard it retold it to someone else, and that person told it to a new group. So the story lived even after the storyteller died.

"Aladdin", after years of being told, was finally written down in Arabia. A Frenchman, Antoine Galland, translated it about 275 years ago into French. His version was part of a very popular book called *A Thousand and One Nights*. Here are some other versions of this old tale you might enjoy:

- "Aladdin and the African Magician", pp. 39—63, in *A Cavalcade of Magicians* by Roger Lancelyn Green (H. Z. Walck 1973).
- *Aladdin*, retold by Jean Lee Latham, illustrated by Pablo Ramirez (Bobbs 1961).
- "The Story of Aladdin, or, The Wonderful Lamp" in *The Arabian Nights* edited by Kate Douglas Wiggin and Nora Smith (Scribner's 1974 c1909).
- *Tales from the Arabian Nights*, illustrated by Brian Wildsmith (Walck 1962).

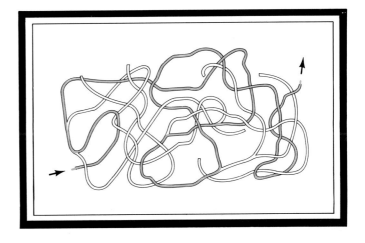